SKY SONGS

Myra Cohn Livingston, *Poet*

Leonard Everett Fisher, *Painter*

Holiday House / New York

COPY 1

For Susanna *and* Alexander
M.C.L.

For Julie, Susan, *and* James
L.E.F.

This book was set in Janson type by
Hallmark Press, Inc.
Color separations were made by Capper, Inc.
It was printed on Moistrite Matte by
Rae Publishing Co., Inc., and bound
by Rae Publishing Co., Inc.
Typography by David Rogers.

The art was prepared with acrylic paint, the
same size as it appears in the book. The
pictures were created on a textured paper and
then peeled from the back of the paper in
preparation for laser light scanning.

Text copyright © 1984 by Myra Cohn Livingston
Illustrations copyright © 1984 by Leonard Everett Fisher
All rights reserved
Printed in the United States of America
First Edition

Library of Congress Cataloging in Publication Data

Livingston, Myra Cohn.
Sky songs.

SUMMARY: Fourteen poems about the various aspects
of the sky such as the moon, clouds, stars, storms,
and sunsets.
1. Sky—Juvenile poetry. 2. Children's poetry,
American. [1. Sky—Poetry. 2. American poetry]
I. Fisher, Leonard Everett, ill. II. Title.
PS3562.I945S5 1984   811'.54   83-12955
ISBN 0-8234-0502-8

Contents

Moon

Why is
the moon always
changing? Sometimes a man
stares down through a window made of
white clouds.

Sometimes
a pale lady,
the dark earth's night mother,
a lace veil over her eyes, smiles
sadly.

How do
they turn themselves
sideways to watch the stars?
What is it they see when they look
away?

Stars

No one
will ever guess
how many billions of
suns live in you. Nobody can
begin

to count
the shining drops
that pour from the Dippers,
the jewels in Orion's belt.
No one

can know
how many eyes
look up to you from fields
and seas in search of a single
lodestar.

The Planets

Across
your dark ocean
the chilled planets journey.
Wanderers of night, they travel
the paths

of their
curving orbits:
Tiny Mercury, Mars,
Venus, bright-ringed Saturn and Earth,
Neptune,

Pluto,
Uranus and
Jupiter, swathed in his
many-colored cloak, his red eye
flashing.

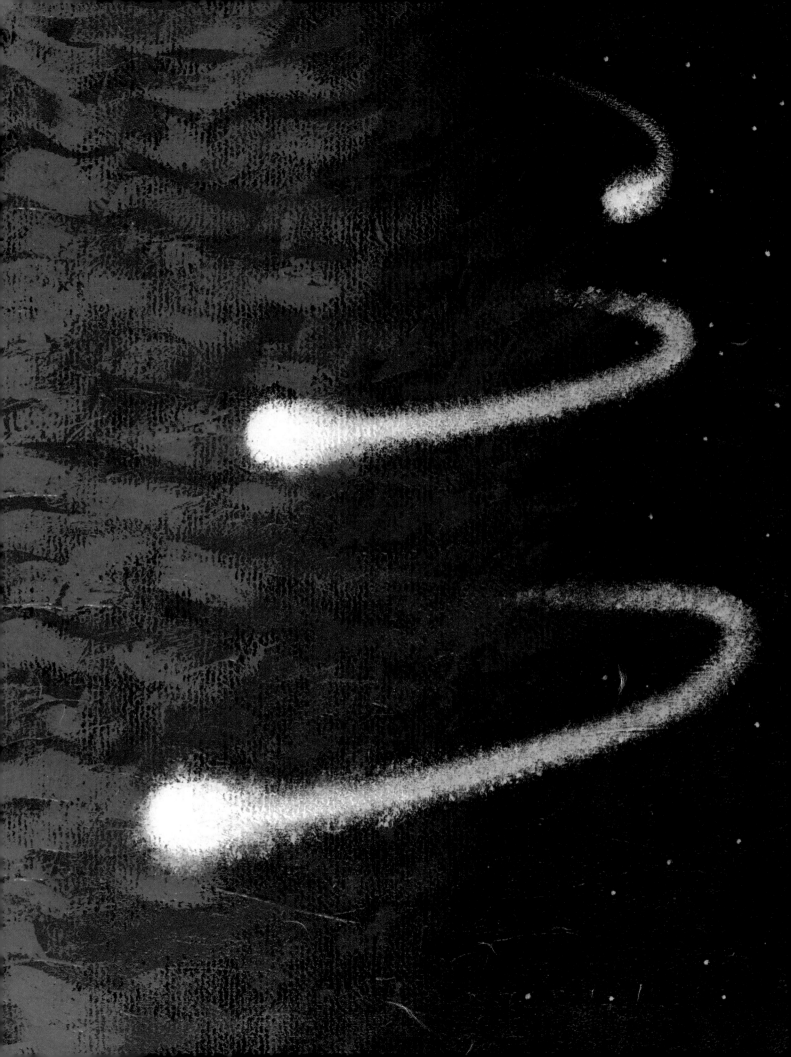

Shooting Stars

Streaking
around the sun,
long-tailed stars, bundled up
in interstellar dust and bright
icy

jackets,
race with shining
meteors, so far off
they will never be seen unless
you shoot

them down
as falling stars,
burning meteorites
or the glowing sunlit tails of
comets.

Morning Sky

Some one
is painting you,
whitewashing over the
black of night and gray of daybreak,
brushing

your top
with palest blue,
coloring your sides pink.
Now, in the first hours of the
morning

you are
earth's astrodome,
floodlit by waking sun,
opening early for the games
of day.

13

Noon

You have
held the hot sun
so long that it has bleached
you white. This morning you carried
it up

to chase
the dark shadows
away, but now you have
pushed it so high that it sits there
gloating,

staring
with one white eye
on the sweltering earth,
laughing at the wildfire it sets
ablaze.

Clouds

Today
strange animals
creep out of white mountains,
stalk each other around in a
dizzy

jumble
of heads and legs,
chase through the silent air,
tumble over themselves as the
paling

sun burns
through their bodies,
and their bleached skeletons,
blown by a rising wind, thin out and
vanish.

Coming Storm

You are
raising a high
roof over earth today;
shingles of gray clouds, thatches of
yellow

straw-light,
enormous folds
of wool batting unroll
as you struggle with the fierce wind
to hide

the sun,
laying dark beams
overhead, and spreading
wet tar to close up the last chinks
of blue.

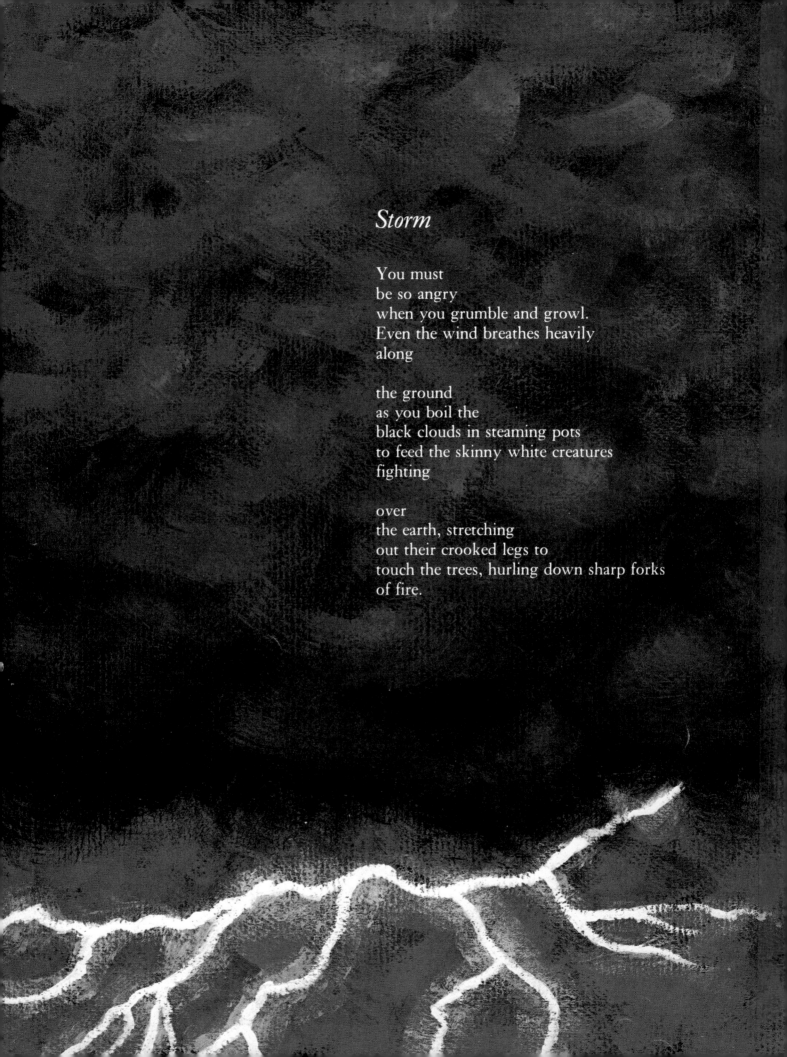

Storm

You must
be so angry
when you grumble and growl.
Even the wind breathes heavily
along

the ground
as you boil the
black clouds in steaming pots
to feed the skinny white creatures
fighting

over
the earth, stretching
out their crooked legs to
touch the trees, hurling down sharp forks
of fire.

21

Tornado

In green
billowing skirts
ruffled with streaks of black,
your clouds crowd too close to the earth,
circling

above
in a strange dance,
while the violent winds
reach down to pick up blowing dust,
whirling

it round
into funnels
that spiral back to you
in the wake of tornado and
cyclone.

Smog

Who is
making you sick?
Choking you with the stench
of smoke that rises up from the
cities

by day,
stifling you with
fumes and vapors that burn
with a brown haze, and poison that
mottles

and plagues
you with cankers,
coughing dust in your face
until your flushing cheeks burn with
fever?

Snow

Trembling
and shivering
in winter, you pull up
blankets of air over your face,
layers

of white
sheets and a great
comforter filled with soft
feathers. But the greedy winds tear
them off,

ripping
them to small bits
that sift through cold clouds and
fall to make a sleeping bag of
snowflakes.

Rain

Some nights
you stay awake
gathering up the rain,
storing it in giant basins
until

they burst
and overflow,
flooding the sleeping earth.
Other times it is a surprise
when you

send down
bright, bouncing drops
that hurry along streets
to dry themselves in a gleaming
rainbow.

Sunset

Now you
dress for evening
in sheer scarves of orange,
veils of pink gauze with lavender
ribbons

trailing
their silver threads.
Frail feathers of bird-wing
brush against your gray gown as you
slowly

enter
a darkened room,
where a mysterious
silence settles as you welcome
sunset.